THE SEARCH FOR SPRING

MOIRA MILLER

Pictures by

IAN DEUCHAR

Dial Books for Young Readers

❖ NEW YORK ❖

There once was a Boy who wanted to know.

How and why was his constant cry, and as his questions grew harder, his parents answered him as best they could.

There came a time when the day of the year stretched toward Summer. Blossoms and butterflies danced. The golden fingers of the sun reached into the darkest corners of the wood, and flowers opened to its touch.

"Now that Summer has come," said the boy's father, "we must shear the sheep of their thick winter coats." He was a farmer for whom each season brought its own tasks.

"If Summer has come," said the boy, "I wonder where Spring has gone?"

"Who knows?" said his father. "For it seems no time since the Autumn, when the hay was stacked to feed the beasts through the Winter."
For once his father, who knew the turning of the seasons
from his beasts and crops, had no answer. And so the boy asked his mother.

"If Summer has come, do you wonder where Spring has gone?"

"I do indeed," said his mother, "for it seems no time since the logs burned bright in the grate and the Christmas pies filled my kitchen with their spice and sweetness." For once his mother, who knew the turning of the seasons from the work of her herb garden and hearth, had no answer.

"It would take a wise man," said the boy's mother, "to tell you where Spring has gone."

The boy, finding that his parents could give him no answer, knew then that the time had come to search for it himself. He took food and drink for the journey, sturdy shoes for the road, and with the blessing of his parents, set off alone.

He found a wise old man living at the top of a tall tower, surrounded by his books.

"Surely," said the boy who wanted to know, "I must find the answer to my search for Spring here."

There were books on the staircase, spiraling to the wise old man's study. There were books in chests and cupboards, in alcoves and long-forgotten corners.

In each book, word and thought, song and poem, slept in silent dusty letters, ready to awaken for the reader.

The wise old man had read each and every word, and written many more of his own. The boy who wanted to know asked him the question his parents could not answer.

"Now that Summer has come," said he, "do you not wonder where Spring has gone?"

"A good question," nodded the wise old man. Together he and the boy pored over books through months and years.

They found many things, and the boy grew in learning all the while. But they could not find the answer to his question. At last the wise old man blew out his candle and peered from the tiny window of the tall tower.

"Spring," he sighed. "I remember Spring. But it has come and gone — I do not know how many times, nor where, nor when." He shook his head in sadness, for he knew that in none of his books would he find the answer.

"Spring," said he, "has gone with the wind."

"Then I must seek the wind," said the boy who wanted to know, "and maybe in my search I will find Spring."

Thanking the wise old man, he set off alone.

The long road led him by a patchwork of shimmering meadows. Poppies and cornflowers nodded gently in the long grass, and bees hummed lazily in the still, sweet air. In the heat of noon the boy knelt to drink in a shady wood where cool water gurgled over shining pebbles.

"What stranger dares to drink from my father's river, and why do you come here?"

Beside him stood a tall young man, finely dressed and carrying a strong wooden staff. The boy smiled.

"I drink," said he, "from the water that no man owns, that falls free as rain on the mountaintops. I am searching for Spring, which has gone with the wind."

"You are trespassing on my father's land," shouted the young man. "He is master here, and Spring—nay Summer, Autumn, and Winter too—are his servants. For him they tend the crops and care for the land."

"Your father may own the land, for a time," said the boy, laughing, "but no man owns the seasons. Nor do they have a master, being more powerful than any man."

"Ignorant fool! No one is more powerful than my father. I will soon show you who is master here."

"I speak the simple truth," said the boy. "Do you think beating me will make it any less true?" He ducked and, seizing a fallen branch, parried the young man's staff as it whistled around his head.

Birds flew off as the clash of sticks and the shouts of the young man and the boy echoed around the sunlit wood. Sometimes it seemed as if the boy would win, and as they fought he grew in strength and courage. But the young man was taller and more forceful. He drove the boy back and back toward the river, lifting his staff to deliver a last sweeping blow.

With a great gust of wind and a crash of thunder, lightning blazed through the trees. A torrent of rain fell upon them, turning the earth to mud beneath their feet.

The young man slipped and, losing his balance, fell into the foaming river.

"Help me! Help me!" he screamed in desperation. The boy, reaching out his stick, pulled the young man to safety. As the two fell, sodden and gasping on the bank, the skies cleared, and the Summer storm passed over.

"It would seem," said the boy, "that the seasons have mastered us both." To that the young man had no answer.

So taking his leave, the boy set off alone in the path of the wild wind, by woodland and river, through a dusty Summer to a golden Autumn. Here and there he would find people in a lonely cottage who shook their heads in wonder at his tale and, giving him food and drink, sent him on his way once more.

The wind became ever more fierce, tossing leaves and twigs before it, and still the boy who wanted to know followed, searching for Spring as the storms gathered around him.

By the bank of a stream, where the bramble bushes grew thick and matted, he found a sheltered cave.

"Here I will spend the night," said he, "with fresh water and a handful of blackberries to go with my last crust so that I may dine like a prince." But as he reached out to pick the sweet berries, a little bird chirped pitifully above his head.

"Take not the fruit, take not the fruit!"

"I am hungry," said the boy, "and so must eat."

The bird set his head on one side, and fixed the
boy with a bright eye.

"Each to his own, each to his own,
If you take the berries, for me there is none."

"Then each to his own indeed," said the boy.
"To the wild birds I leave the wild fruits.
I will eat of the bread that man has baked,
from the wheat that man has grown."

"Share and share," chirped the bird. "Share and share."

"Again you are right, little bird." The boy broke bread
for the bird and gathered a handful of berries for himself,
and together they shared a meal and the shelter of the cave.

The following morning the boy told of his search for Spring.
The bird listened, then flew off, beckoning and calling as he went.
"Feather and wing, feather and wing,
Must help Adam's child to seek the Spring."
The boy followed, by forest and field, over mountain and
moorland. The wild winds roared and the trees bowed down
their heads, laying a path of leaves at his feet.
Always he followed where the wind and the little bird led
in his search for Spring. And as he followed, the wind grew colder,
bringing sleet and snow.

The boy trudged on by paths of ice, through deep drifts.

He strode across lakes and rivers, ringing like crystal to his steps, where waterfalls hung frozen, enchanted in the biting air.

He huddled at night beside a fire whose tiny sparks flashed as brilliantly as the stars in darkest space. And still there seemed no end to the search for Spring.

As the boy grew in tenderness, the little bird, held safe and warm inside his jerkin, cheered him onward.

"Seek and find, seek and find,
Go search for Spring on Winter's wind."

There came a day when the rivers began at last to stretch and turn in their icy beds.

The boy singing and the bird fluttering around his head, they came down into a broad valley where melting snow sparkled diamond-bright in the fields. A thread of smoke trickled from the chimney of a lonely farmhouse. In the garden a woman was scattering grain for her birds.

"A fine day," she called, "for a traveler on a long road."

"Long it is," said the boy. "I have been many places and walked many miles in my search for Spring." The woman threw down her basket.

"Then seek you no farther," said she. "Your quest is ended—for Spring is here, and even now around you."

Beneath the trees, where the snow had melted, lay a patch of dark, sweet-smelling earth. Through the soft green moss a tiny bunch of fragile flowers — snowdrops and golden winter aconites — raised their heads to the sunsparkle of the early year.

The little bird sang for joy in the tree above their heads as the boy and the woman stared in silent wonder.

"In truth my search is ended," said he, "I have at last found Spring, and it was always here."

"That is so indeed," said the woman. "But I wonder where my boy has gone?"

First published in the United States 1988
by Dial Books for Young Readers,
A Division of NAL Penguin Inc.
2 Park Avenue
New York, New York 10016
Published in Great Britain
by Methuen Children's Books Ltd
Text copyright © 1988 by Moira Miller
Pictures copyright © 1988 by Ian Deuchar
First Edition
US
1 3 5 7 9 10 8 6 4 2

Library of Congress Cataloging in Publication Data
Miller, Moira. The search for spring.
Summary: Mystified by the change of seasons,
a curious boy sets out to find where Spring has gone.
[1. Seasons—Fiction.] I. Deuchar, Ian, ill.
II. Title
PZ7.M6313Se 1988   [E]   86-32898
ISBN 0-8037-0445-3